This book is dedicated to my biggest, proudest achievements, my beautiful boys, Coan and Kashyn. I love you more than any words can express.

It was an exciting day in Dinosaur Village,

3 eggs were about to hatch.

Mummy and Daddy Dinosaur watched impatiently,

over their precious clutch.

Their family would finally be growing,

they could not wait to see,

the pitter patter of little feet,

how happy they will be.

Mummy imagined her proud moment,

when she showed off her children to all.

'Oooooo, aaaaah, how adorable' they would say,

'What a beautiful family!' they would call.

Out came the sun, to wake up the day,

everyone in Dinosaur Village was buzzing.

The eggs were moving, it was so exciting,

anytime now they would hear them tapping.

A crack, a wriggle, a stretch and a wiggle,

one by one they popped out.

The first one got an ooooo, the second an aaaahhhh,

but the last received no admiring shout.

The third dinosaur was different you see, and not at all like his brothers.

'What are those things on his head, what are those things on his shoulders,

he has a tail like a whale', sniggered the others.

Mummy and Daddy Dinosaur looked most upset and very sadly thought,

'How rude and unkind the others are, to laugh and point and taunt.

Davy, Dexter AND Dygon Dinosaur are all our beautiful sons,

what did it matter to any of them, if Dygon was a different one.'

Being different to the others was no reason to be snubbed,

so Mummy hugged him extra tight to show how much he was loved.

Dygon was different, his Mummy had to agree,

but the others shouldn't treat him so unkindly.

Davy and Dexter Dinosaur quickly realised,

how different Dygon was to them, even in size.

Play was ruined when he was involved, he was clumsy, careless and slow,

he wasn't wanted in their games, Dygon would always know.

But Mummy would make them include Dygon,

'he's your little brother', she would say.

But they teased him and mocked him and made him feel sad,

so Dygon found it better to stay away.

He stayed close to his Mummy and Daddy,

where he felt safe, loved and protected,

and only saw his brothers at meal and bedtimes,

but even then, they made him feel rejected.

As the months went by and they all grew bigger,

'he is getting weirder', Dygon's brothers would snigger.

It made him sad because he dreamed of being the same,

popular and loved, and always included in their game.

Then one day, while the whole family was eating dinner,

Dygon felt a burning tickle in his nose.

He let out a sneeze, that brought him to his knees,

and out shot a bolt of fire, everyone froze.

It burnt Dexter's hair and made him cry out in despair,

but Dygon couldn't stop his sneezing.

'ACHOO ACHOO ACHOO!' he roared,

and burnt holes in the furniture, walls and ceiling.

Mummy and Daddy were incredibly shocked,

what was happening to their son?

Scared and alone, they didn't know what to do,

but they had to protect Dygon and everyone.

They decided to move Dygon to a different cave,

where he would stay with just his Daddy.

Mummy would visit him every day,

to ensure he wouldn't feel too lonely.

Dygon was so sad, he wept long, silent, hot tears.

He didn't want to stay away from his home for the rest of his years.

He thought of ways to make it better, but none came to mind,

he needed everyone to know he didn't mean to be unkind.

Dygon Dinosaur hated the new cave,

it was dark, damp and gloomy.

But later that day, as Dygon sobbed away,

he heard a voice say, 'Don't be sad, Roomy'.

He turned around in fright, and adjusted his sight,

to see a creature suddenly take flight.

It landed near Dygon and introduced himself,

'I'm Berty the Bat, I just came down from that shelf.

I've been watching you being sad, so down I flew,

can we be friends as I live here too?'

Dygon was thrilled, he was no longer alone,

he had finally found a best friend all of his own.

They talked about their dreams and hung out all day,

Dygon finally had a chance to be able to play.

Their favourite game was 'Splat the Bat', a game of power and might,

where Dygon had to use his tail to smack Berty in flight.

More months went by and Dygon grew bigger,

and a lot more different, Mummy thought.

Berty saw it too, how Dygon's shoulder flaps grew,

how would he ever get the acceptance he sought?

But on the day Dygon and his brothers turned one,

his Mummy and Daddy planned a huge party for everyone.

There would be cakes, balloons, and lots of fun and games,

Dygon was excited to be involved and treated the same.

Berty helped him get ready, excited to be included as well,

when all of a sudden, they heard an almighty yell.

'That's Mummy,' said Dygon, 'she sounds very scared.

And what's that flapping sound, like a very big bird.'

Without a second thought, Dygon ran outside,

the sun so bright, he had to first hide his eyes.

He saw a huge winged creature, circling the sky,

Dygon stood in front of his family, his hands spread high.

There was complete silence, followed by gasps of 'whoa!',

as the other dinosaurs saw Dygon's beautiful wings flow.

Even the winged creature looked down in utter shock,

the creature below looked like he belonged in his flock.

He swooped down to Dygon and blew out a flame,

this was going to be one spectacular game.

The fire melted the birthday cake and burnt all the bunting,

the dinosaurs screamed and ran but the creature continued his hunting.

Dygon opened his mouth and fired right back,

but the creature always managed to evade the attack.

'Flap your wings, Dygon, you can fly,' Berty had to shout,

'You've got to get up there and smack that fella out.'

Dygon started to flap his wings, slowly at first,

then faster and faster until his feet left the dirt.

He bent his legs and pushed himself off the ground,

he was a natural and with Berty's help, was soon swooping around.

A huge battle of wings and tails and fire lit up the sky,

Dygon felt incredible power and fought with great pride.

The fight continued like a firework display,

both Dygon and the creature refusing to give it away.

'Think of our game,' Berty shouted at the right moment,

Dygon flicked his tail like a whale and swatted his opponent.

The creature fell to the ground, clearly defeated,

Dygon swooped back down, ready to repeat it.

'Who are you,' the creature asked admiringly,

'I'm Dygon the Dinosaur,' Dygon said proudly.

The creature opened his mouth to laugh with a wheeze,

'No, you are not, you are a dragon just like me.'

'I AM A DINOSAUR,' shouted Dygon with anger and pride,

but he had a funny feeling, a strange knowing inside.

'Look at your magnificent wings, you're a fire-breathing wonder.

Surely you knew you are different to them, didn't you even ponder?'

Dygon looked around, of course this dragon was right,

he was different, even if he wished with all his might.

The dragon rose in the air, introducing himself as Drake,

'I know not to challenge YOU again, great fight there little mate.'

And as he flew away and Dygon's sad face went out of view,

he thought 'what a hero Dygon is, I wonder if he knew?'

As soon as Drake was out of sight, the entire village erupted,

with chants, cheers and hip hip hoorays, it wasn't what Dygon expected.

They lifted him up high in the air, 'OUR BRAVE HERO' they shouted,

thanking him for saving them and finally making him feel wanted.

His Mummy and Daddy were ever so proud, of their incredible little boy,

to see everyone finally show him such love, filled them with utmost joy.

Dygon was so happy, more than he had ever been,

his 1st birthday party was the biggest celebration Dino Village had seen.

Dygon's life changed from that amazing day,

he was everyone's favourite and was always asked to play.

Berty was always at his side, enjoying all the sights,

as Dygon explored the outside world, taking many flights.

Dygon knew he was different, but that was okay,

he was an important member of his village, in a very special way.

He put on fire shows, and gave rides on his tail,

and took the villagers on many trips, through the skies they would sail.

He met other dragons on the way, including his buddy Drake,

Who taught him all the amazing things dragons could undertake.

Dygon finally felt accepted, included, and privileged, and remained the

nicest, kindest member of Dinosaur Village.

THE END

What did you learn?

Q1. What are the names of Dygon's two brothers?

Q2. How was Dygon different from the other dinosaurs in the village?

Q3. Who was Dygon's best friend?

Q4. What favourite game did Dygon and Berty play?

Q5. Name 5 different dinosaurs?

Q6. Why is it important to be kind to everyone?

Have a go at drawing Dygon below.

Acknowledgments

Thank you, Universe, for your kindness, your miracles, and your blessings every day.

To my darling Dadikins and Mumzi, thank you for teaching me, by being who you are, kindness, generosity, compassion, to be grateful and full of love.

To my precious husband, thank you for always believing in me, for loving me the way you do, and supporting me, on this new journey and always.

To my beautiful boys, you are my compass.

To my wonderful sisters, my Muskateers, my voices of reason and endless encouragement (or is it nagging?), thank you.

To my dearest family and friends, who always show me such love and support, thank you.

To my unbelievably talented 14year old (at the time) illustrator, Thashen. I am in awe of your gift. Thank you for bringing my story to life so beautifully. I am your biggest fan.

To dearest, Salosh, the captain of my artist. I am so grateful for your dedication and commitment to this project, and your patience.

To my nephew Kia, you played a huge part in making this happen. Thank you darling.

To my adorable friend, Gareth, thank you for lighting a fire under me and cheering me on. I will never forget how thrilled you were when I finished the first draft. I finally saw it through and thought of you often along the way.

To Linz, thank you for being my critical friend and suggesting 'less words, more pictures.'

To Harmeet and Rick, thank you for also being my critical friends. Your advice was invaluable.

Printed in Great Britain
by Amazon

60650332R00015